The Last Portal

D0682290

522 433 28 6

Collect all the Charmseekers -

www.charmseekers.co.uk

CHARMSEEKERS: BOOK THIRTEEN

The Last Portal

Georgie Adams

Illustrated by Gwen Millward

Orion
Children's Books

First published in Great Britain in 2009
by Orion Children's Books
Reissued 2012 by Orion Children's Books
a division of the Orion Publishing Group Ltd
Orion House
5 Upper St Martin's Lane
London WC2H 9EA
An Hachette UK Company

1 3 5 7 9 8 6 4 2

Text copyright © Georgie Adams 2009
Illustrations copyright © Gwen Millward 2009

The right of Georgie Adams and Gwen Millward to be
identified as the author and illustrator
respectively of this work has been asserted.

All rights reserved. No part of this publication may be
reproduced, stored in a retrieval system, or transmitted,
in any form or by any means, electronic, mechanical,
photocopying, recording or otherwise, without the prior
permission of Orion Children's Books.

The Orion Publishing Group's policy is to use papers
that are natural, renewable and recyclable products and
made from wood grown in sustainable forests. The logging
and manufacturing processes are expected to conform to
the environmental regulations of the country of origin.

A catalogue record for this book is available from the British Library.

ISBN 978 1 4440 0301 7

Printed and bound by
CPI Group (UK) Ltd, Croydon, CR0 4YY

www.orionbooks.co.uk
www.charmseekers.co.uk

For Fiona Kennedy — my editorial guide and mentor on the quest — with much love and appreciation.

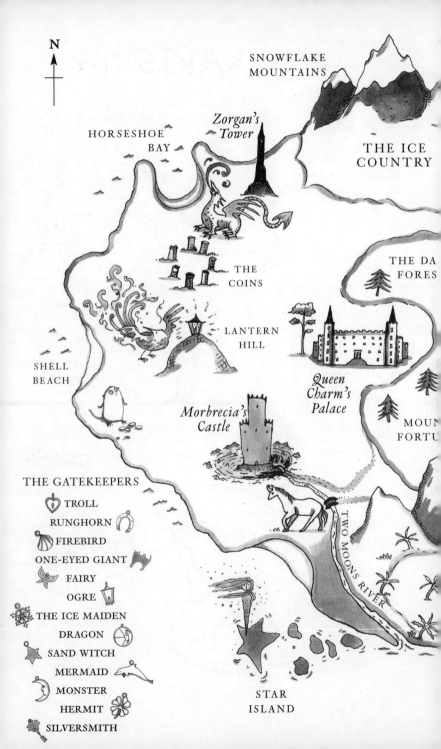

The Thirteen Charms of Karisma

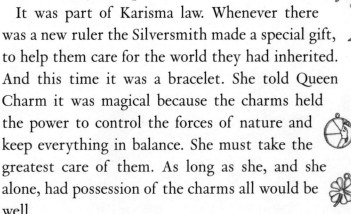

When Charm became queen of Karisma, the wise and beautiful Silversmith made her a precious gift. It was a bracelet. On it were fastened thirteen silver amulets, which the Silversmith called 'charms', in honour of the new queen.

It was part of Karisma law. Whenever there was a new ruler the Silversmith made a special gift, to help them care for the world they had inherited. And this time it was a bracelet. She told Queen Charm it was magical because the charms held the power to control the forces of nature and keep everything in balance. She must take the greatest care of them. As long as she, and she alone, had possession of the charms all would be well.

And so it was, until the bracelet was stolen by a spider, and fell into the hands of Zorgan, the magician. Then there was chaos!

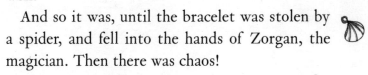

One

One Saturday evening, shortly before her birthday, Sesame was at home with her grandmother, Lossy, watching television. She was engrossed in a programme about rescuing orphan orangutans. She thought the babies looked adorable, playing with their carers in a reserve.

"I wish *I* could look after an orangutan," she said, and suddenly a vision of Fig popped into her head.

He was the tiny tunganora* she'd
rescued, when she'd gone to
Karisma for the first time.
Sesame had last seen Fig and
his mother, Hob, after the Feast
of the Stolen Goblet,** and she
wondered how they were.

Lossy glanced at her granddaughter sitting on the
sofa cuddling her cats, Chips and Pins. She knew
how much Sesame loved animals and the TV
programme had given Lossy an idea. I'll go online
when Sesame's gone to bed and find out more about
it, she thought. Then she quickly changed the
subject.

"I expect Nic and Jodie are having a lovely
evening," she remarked casually.

"Mm," said Sesame. She sounded
enthusiastic. "Dad says he's going
to ask Jodie to marry him tonight.
He's bought a ring. I saw it
yesterday. It's gorgeous!"

* *
* Tunganora – a small ape-like animal with long, pink
shaggy hair, which feeds on the blue-spotted leaves of
the tuntree
**The Feast of the Stolen Goblet – gribblers perform
this ceremony, in which a powerful potion of leaves is
sipped from a goblet, reputed to be stolen from Agapogo

4

Lossy smiled. Sesame's mother, Poppy, had died when she was a baby and during the past year, Lossy had noticed a growing bond between Sesame and her riding teacher, Jodie Luck. A while ago, when Nic had asked Sesame how she *might* feel about having Jodie as her stepmother, she'd replied without hesitation: "Wicked!"

⁂

Next day, Sesame, Nic and Lossy were discussing ideas for Sesame's birthday party. It was just two weeks' away and this year it fell at half-term, on Friday the thirteenth.

"Could I have a disco with a real DJ?" Sesame asked.

"Sounds great," said Nic.

"What about the noise?" Lossy said. "We don't want to upset Mrs Adams next door."

"If we give her plenty of warning, I'm sure she'll understand," Nic said. "I know a super DJ called Spinner Shindigs and we can have a marquee in the garden."

"*Thanks* Dad," said Sesame, her eyes shining with delight. "I've got loads of friends I'd like to ask. It'll be the best party ever! Don't worry, Gran. I'll go and see Mrs Adams. She's good fun. I'll invite her too."

Chips and Pins caught Sesame's excited mood and chased each other round the furniture.

"Okay," she said. "I won't forget you!"

Sesame got busy straightaway. First she wrote a guest list (quite a long one), then she designed and printed party invitations on her computer.

Please come to my
Birthday Disco Party
At Home on Friday 13th
7pm until late.
RSVP Sesame Brown
email: seekerSes@zoom.com

So, early on Monday morning Sesame was in the playground handing out invitations. There was one each for her special friends – Maddy Webb (her *best* friend), Gemma Green and Liz Robinson – and Sesame had specially remembered to invite Hayley, a new girl in her class.

"Thank you," said Hayley, her sea-blue eyes sparkling. She wore her golden blonde hair swept back with a hairband, like Sesame. "I love disco dancing!"

Sesame and Maddy sat near Hayley in class and they'd liked her at once. One breaktime, while they were chatting, Hayley told them a little about herself; she had a brown-and-white puppy called Snoopy, played the flute and loved collecting jewellery. When they heard about the jewellery, Sesame and Maddy exchanged glances; if only Hayley knew *they* collected magical charms! Maybe one day, Sesame thought, I'll tell her about our Charmseekers club.

Before long, Sesame was surrounded by a gaggle of girls, all chattering about her party and what they were going to wear.

When Olivia Pike came along, Sesame surprised everyone by giving her an invitation too. The whole school knew Sesame and Olivia were not the best of friends! But that was before an incident at Jodie's stables, when Sesame caught Olivia's runaway pony. Ever since, the two girls had been on friendlier terms. Maddy stared at Sesame open-mouthed.

"Wha—" she began.

"It's okay," whispered Sesame. "I'll explain later."

Olivia looked really pleased to be invited.

"Thanks, Ses," she said. "A disco with a real DJ? Wow. It'll be SO cool!"

Two

One morning on Mount Fortuna, the Silversmith wakes early, sensing there is something special about today. She throws off the coverlet, wraps herself in a gossamer robe and crosses the room to her window.

It is dawn. The fiery sun is beginning to rise over Mount Fortuna and already she can hear birds singing. The Silversmith looks at her calendar and sees that it is the thirteenth day of the thirteenth mede* of Quorus.

* * * * * * * * * *

*Mede – month

"Of course," she murmurs. "Midsummer's Day. The most magical day of the year!"

Her thoughts fly to her Seeker, and for a reason she cannot explain, the Silversmith is sure this day will be special for Sesame too. She brushes her long, silvery hair, dresses, then hurries downstairs to her workshop to look at the thirteen magical candles. One by one, twelve candles have flickered and gone out – each one bearing the name of a precious charm: the heart, horseshoe, shell, cat, butterfly, snowflake, lantern, coin, star, dolphin, moon and, most recently, the lucky four-leafed clover. These charms, she knows, are safe with her Seeker in the Outworld.* Only one candle remains burning – a glowing beacon for the lost silver key.

"Last but not least," she says. "Sesame must find the thirteenth charm to complete the magical bracelet. Only then will order be restored to Karisma. The time has come for her to return . . ."

* *

✱ Outworld – the name Karismans call our world

The Silversmith lights fragrant tinder-sticks of mystica* that fill the room with a spicy-sweet aroma. Placing her fingertips to her temples, she breathes deeply, then focuses her thoughts on Sesame, her jewellery box and the charm bracelet. Soon she is in a trance, summoning her mystic powers to transport herself – far beyond the boundaries of Karisma – to the Outworld!

* *
*Mystica – an aromatic plant, native to Karisma. The petals produce a sweet smell when burned

11

Three

Sesame's birthday, Friday the thirteenth, dawned bright and sunny.

"It's going to be a fab day!" she sang, dancing round her room with Alfie, her teddy, swinging him round and round. Racing downstairs in her pyjamas, she found her dad and Lossy having breakfast in the kitchen. The post had arrived and there was a pile of birthday cards waiting for her on the table.

"Happy birthday, Ses," said Nic, hugging her tight.

Lossy gave her granddaughter a kiss. "Just think, you're a whole year older!" she said.

Sesame munched her muesli and opened her cards at the same time. There was one from her aunt in Scotland, enclosing some birthday money.

"Brill!" exclaimed Sesame. "I've been saving up for the new Crystal Chix album for ages. Now I've got enough money to buy it."

"Here's my present," said Lossy, handing her a large, flat package.

"Ooo," said Sesame, opening it with care. "I wonder what's inside?" She took out a glossy brochure, a photograph and a certificate.

"Wow!" gasped Sesame, her big brown eyes open wide with excitement. "I've adopted a baby orangutan called Kee-Kee. Look, Dad, here's his photo. He's gorgeous. Oh, Gran, *thank* you!"

"What a fantastic idea," said Nic.

"I thought you'd be pleased," said Lossy.

Orangutan Appeal

CERTIFICATE OF APPRECIATION

Kee-Kee has been adopted by
Sesame Brown
In recognition of your kind
support and sponsorship.

Signed

Director,
Orangutan Rehabilitation Centre

For the next few minutes, Sesame's head was buried in the brochure reading about Kee-Kee. He was being cared for in a rehabilitation centre, just like the one she'd seen on TV.

LUCKY KEE-KEE!

Kee-Kee arrived in our Rehabilitation Centre on Friday the thirteenth – a lucky day for the orphan orangutan. She was found by one of our rangers, hungry and searching for food. Kee-Kee's mother was killed by contractors, who had been clearing the rainforest for palm oil development. Kee-Kee is four years old with long red hair. She weighs fourteen kilos and is very affectionate, full of energy and loves climbing trees. One of her favourite pastimes is having a bath. She splashes around and loves being cuddled, while she's dried in a towel.

Kee-Kee will be looked after in our centre until she's ready to be released into the rainforest, where she will continue to be protected.

Nic glanced at his watch and gave Lossy a knowing smile.

"Er, Ses," he began. "I'm afraid *my* present was a bit awkward to wrap—"

Sesame rolled her eyes.

"Dad, I don't mind. What is it?"

"It's . . . I mean . . . he's waiting for you at Jodie's stables," said Nic.

It took a moment or two for Sesame to take in what her dad had just said. She hardly dared believe what she *thought* he was saying.

"D-a-d—?"

"Get dressed for riding," said Nic. "We don't want to keep *your* pony waiting!"

Sesame sat in the car in a daze, repeating over and over again in her head the words – *your* pony!

She was still wondering if it was just a dream as Nic parked the car at the stables. Jodie was waiting in the yard with Silver, tacked up and ready to ride, and fluttering from his bridle was a gold rosette:

Sesame
Happy
Birthday!
Love,
Dad xx

Sesame was so excited she wanted to cry and hug them all at the same time. She flung her arms around Silver's neck, then hugged Nic and Jodie together.

"Here," said Jodie, eventually disentangling herself to produce a neatly-wrapped parcel. "You'll need this. Happy Birthday, Ses!"

A few minutes later, Sesame was proudly wearing a smart new riding hat.

"Thank you, Jodie!" she said, and gave her a kiss.

For a while, Nic and Jodie watched Sesame riding confidently round the sand school; and when Nic took a photograph, Jodie remarked:

"Sesame and Silver. They're made for each other."

Nic turned to her. Jodie was wearing his engagement ring and the diamonds sparkled in the sunlight.

"So are we," he said happily. "Now, I must go. There's a lot to do to get ready for the party."

Jodie blew him a kiss.

"We'll be back soon to give a hand," she said.

* * *

Two hours later, Sesame and Jodie arrived to find a bright pink van parked outside the house. It had Spinner Shindigs' Mobile Disco painted on the side.

17

"Ooo!" squealed Sesame. She had caught sight of a good-looking young man in skinny jeans and dark glasses, carrying headphones, speakers and sound equipment down the garden path. "He must be Spinner Shindigs, the DJ."

"Right," said Jodie. "And there's your dad halfway up the apple tree!"

Nic and a friend were busy stringing lights in the branches. He waved to them and nearly lost his balance. Jodie shook her head and laughed.

"I'm going to help Lossy with the food," she told Sesame. "You go and change. I'll see you later."

"Okay," said Sesame. "I must look glam for my party!"

She raced upstairs to her room. The first thing she saw was a photograph, propped on her dressing table – the one Nic had taken earlier.

"Silver, my very own pony," she said, still hardly able to believe it. Lying next to the photo was a picture of Kee-Kee, her adopted orangutan. She was proud of her too. Quickly she put the photos down, then opened her wardrobe door.

"What *am* I going to wear?" she said.

Her bedroom floor was soon strewn with clothes, shoes and accessories – silky dresses, mini skirts, jeans, tee-shirts, sparkly tops and sequinned sandals, not to mention the entire contents of her make-up bag!

Glitter nail polish, lip gloss, body glow and dazzle dust – to name but a few – littered the carpet. Eventually she decided on her bright red top with a sparkly heart,* purple mini-shorts and shimmering tights. Then she sat on her bed and put on her favourite necklace – the locket with pictures of her parents inside.

Unexpectedly, a terrifying image of Zorgan the magician suddenly swam into her head; she vividly recalled what happened the last time she was in Karisma. Somehow (she didn't know exactly how) her locket had saved her from Zorgan's powerful jinx. The jinx had struck like a thunderbolt and knocked her to the floor. There had been a blinding *flash*. An ear-splitting CRACK! She guessed the jinx must have bounced off her locket and hit Zorgan, because the next thing she knew, he'd disappeared in a puff of smoke. She could still hear his wail ringing in her ears.

As Sesame held her locket now, she was aware of a tingling sensation in her fingers. It was a familiar feeling, and it nearly always meant something extraordinary was about to happen! Butterflies

* *
* Do you remember what happened when Sesame first saw it in **Tip Tops**? Read about her exciting adventure in Book One: *The Queen's Bracelet*

tickled her tummy and something compelled her to reach for her jewellery box. It contained the precious charm bracelet. She opened the lid, took out the bracelet and admired the twelve magical charms fastened to the silver band.

"Only one charm still missing," she said. "I must find the key!"

Outside, Spinner Shindigs was testing his speakers. Sesame heard rhythmic beats and recognised the unmistakable sound of the Crystal Chix. But then she heard another voice singing and was sure it wasn't the CD. The sweet sound echoed inside her head like a thousand tinkling bells.

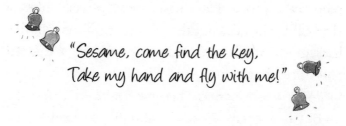

"Sesame, come find the key,
Take my hand and fly with me!"

Sesame closed her eyes and shook her head. Was she hearing things? When she opened them again, she saw her room bathed in the soft, golden glow of candlelight and she was floating above her bed! Slowly she drifted up, up, up, still holding tight to the charm bracelet, until the ceiling melted away into a mist of tiny, twinkling stars . . .

As if in a dream, Sesame felt someone take her gently by the hand. Through a shimmering haze, she saw a young woman with long, silvery hair and thought the beautiful stranger looked familiar. Sesame struggled to remember where she might have seen her before.

"Who are you?" said Sesame.

But her words were lost and all she heard was a tinkling echo.

"... fly ... fly ... fly with me!"

* Four *

The dawn sky was a blaze of pink, blue and gold as Sesame and the Silversmith drifted on a sunbeam, towards Mount Fortuna. They landed, light as thistledown, outside the Silversmith's workshop.

"Come in," she invited Sesame, opening the door. "We have much to talk about."

Still shaken and bewildered, Sesame followed her inside. Everywhere she looked were curious ornaments, carvings and sculptures; there were star charts, moon charts and drawings of the magical charms; neatly arranged on a workbench was an assortment of tools and, over by the window, was a row of candles – but only one was burning.

"Please, tell me who you are," said Sesame.

"I'm the Silversmith," the young woman replied.

"Are you a . . . gatekeeper?" asked Sesame.

"In a way," said the Silversmith with a smile. "I'm the last portal. I had to bring you here to find the thirteenth charm."

"The key!" said Sesame. "Look, I have the bracelet with me."

Sesame opened her palm and the Silversmith gasped.

"Oh," she cried. "The precious charms! How wonderful to see them again. Do you know, I made the bracelet for Queen Charm here in this workshop. I can't wait to tell Her Majesty. She's been longing for its return, since the day it was stolen. Today is a holiday to celebrate Midsummer's Day. It would be perfect to return the bracelet to her on this special day. Charm is looking forward to meeting you."

"I'd love to meet *her*," said Sesame. "After I've found the key."

"We're depending on you," said the Silversmith. "Let me show you something."

24

Sesame followed her across the room to the window.

"These are *magic* candles," said the Silversmith, and she explained how they worked. Sesame noticed the one remaining candle bore the name of the key.  "I'll find it," she promised. "Sesame Brown will track it down!"

The Silversmith gave her a look filled with warmth and affection. She had chosen well. Her Seeker would see her quest through to the end.

"I see you're wearing your locket," she said.

"Yes," said Sesame. "It has pictures of my parents. I'll show you."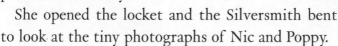

She opened the locket and the Silversmith bent to look at the tiny photographs of Nic and Poppy.

"No wonder it means so much to you," said the Silversmith gently. "I'm sorry Zorgan and his pixies gave you so much trouble."

"You know about—" began Sesame.

25

"I have . . . special powers," said the Silversmith. "I have been able to communicate with you through your locket. I knew the instant you were parted from it and I felt a terrible jolt when Zorgan's jinx struck it."

"What *did* happen?" asked Sesame, amazed the Silversmith knew so much about her.

"It rebounded," said the Silversmith simply. "You were very lucky to escape unharmed. Your locket saved you and destroyed the magician.* A jinx striking silver is exceptionally powerful, you see. When it bounced back and hit Zorgan, he didn't stand a chance. Karisma is well rid of that vermy** magician, and we have you to thank for our good fortune."

Just then they heard a strange noise outside the window. *Whoop-whoop-whoop!* Sesame knew she'd heard it before and when she looked, there were Hob and Fig!

"SESAME!" cried the tunganoras, jumping up and down with delight.

* *
* Do you remember what happened? You can read about Zorgan's dramatic end in Book Twelve: *Zorgan and the Gorsemen*
**Vermy – miserable worm

26

Sesame and the Silversmith ran outside to greet them. Hob was carrying a box, which Sesame recognised at once.

"My lunch box!" she exclaimed. "I left it in the jungle. How did you find it?"

"It's a long story," said Hob. "We were looking for food near Butterfly Bay—"

"—And we saw this great . . . BIG . . . enormous Plod-puss-opussy!" broke in Fig excitedly.

Hob, Sesame and the Silversmith laughed.

"I think you *may* have seen a Plodopus," * said the Silversmith.

"Anyway," said Hob, "Fig came across your lunch box. It was very useful for carrying the goblet."

"Goblet?" queried the Silversmith.

"The one the gribblers stole from Agapogo," ** said Sesame, opening the lid. "I took it away from them and now Hob and Fig have brought it to you."

* *
* **Plodopus** – this plant-eating dinosaur is believed to be a close relative of Diplodocus, which lived in the Outworld millions of years ago
** **Agapogo** – a favourite name for dragons, which means 'to spit fire'

27

"How wonderful!" said the Silversmith, holding up the fine silver goblet. "We shall return it to Agapogo straightaway. The Silver Pool is not far from here."

Hob and Fig were tired; they had walked all the way from the jungle. Fig was sucking his paws and Sesame knew it was a sure sign he was hungry. Suddenly an image of her adopted orangutan, Kee-Kee, swam into her head. She felt responsible for the tunganoras; they had kept their promise to look after the goblet, now she must help them.

"Are there any tuntrees around here?" she asked the Silversmith. "Hob and Fig are hungry."

The tunganoras looked at the Silversmith hopefully with their wide, appealing eyes.

"I've got some in my garden," she said. "Come along. You have done well. You're welcome to stay as long as you like. You'll be safe and there's plenty of food!"

Five

It had been a while since anyone had seen a gribbler* in the Dark Forest. The vile, fat, foul-smelling gribblers – their bodies covered in blobby warts, their sharp teeth a disgusting shade of yellow – had been frightened off by the Tree Spirits, soon after the Feast of the Stolen Goblet.

Three gribblers, Varg, Gorz and Bod had squelched across a marshy area known as The Swamps and reached the coast. Very few trees grew here and the gribblers were miserable – that is to say they were more miserable than usual, because gribblers are usually bad-tempered. At dusk one evening, as the light was fading, the biggest gribbler, Varg, was in a particularly disagreeable mood.

* *
*Gribbler – extremely unpleasant goblin-like creature with yellow teeth and bad breath

29

"Can't shee a shoshege in thish light," he said, squinting his hooded eyes and spraying his companions with slime.

"Can't find anything to eat in this place," grumbled Gorz. "I'm so hungry I could eat worms!"

"I just did," said Bod, the youngest. "I can feel them wriggling in my tummy."

The three had just reached the end of a narrow strip of land called Key Point, which jutted out into the sea. If the gribblers had any sense (which they didn't) they might have caught some fish, but they were far too stupid to think of it. Instead, they continued to peer at the ground looking for morsels of food, until Bod saw something silvery, glinting in a pool of moonlight. He stopped to pick it up.

"Washat?" said Varg, snatching it from him.

"I found it," protested Bod. "It's mine!"

Varg cuffed him round the ear.

"It's only a key," said Gorz, squinting at it with his piggy eyes.

"Itch a *charm*, shtoopid," said Varg, dribbling goo from his fangs. "Morbreeesha told ush to look out for charms, didn't sheee? We mush take thish to the princhess!"

An idea slowly formed inside Gorz's head. He drew back his lizard lips, showing yellowing teeth, and grinned.

"Maybe she'll give us a reward," he said.

"Well, let's go," said Bod.

But the gribblers had wandered into the territory of the Urchins – five skinny boys with slime-green bodies and flat, webbed feet called Tyke, Gumba, Lumsy, Lug and Fiz. The urchins spent their time beachcombing and regarded anything left lying about (which they called left-behindings) as their property.

"What have you got there?" demanded the tallest urchin, Tyke, appearing out of nowhere. "Who are you anyway?"

"None of your bishness," growled Varg, quickly hiding the key behind his back.

The urchins ducked to avoid the slime spray and held their noses too. The gribblers stank of rotting fish and the smell was unbearable.

"It is if you're stealing our left-behindings," said Gumba.

"Don't care if we are," said Varg.

"What are we waiting for?" asked Gorz.

"RUN!" cried Bod.

So the gribblers ran (hoping they were going in the direction of Morbrecia's castle) and the urchins chased them across The Swamps.

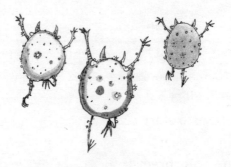

Six

Morbrecia's castle was crammed with books. After Zorgan's defeat, she had lost no time in raiding the magician's magnificent library. Morbrecia had loaded her carriage with spell books, then her servants had spent days putting them on bookshelves; and when those were full, they'd piled them on the floor. The princess couldn't wait to start making magic!

Most of Zorgan's books were for experienced magicians. Morbrecia was a beginner so, not surprisingly, she had a few unfortunate mishaps. Making potions, for example, is a bit like cooking. You follow a recipe, or the dish may be ruined. It takes time to become a good cook and it's the same with sorcery. If you make a mistake with magic, the results are disastrous.

33

The first leather-bound volume Morbrecia opened was A Pot Full of Potions. She'd selected a potion and, in her hurry, hadn't bothered to weigh the ingredients. A pinch of this, a handful of that – before long, Morbrecia had mixed a disgusting green and slimy brew. Alarmingly, the pongy potion refilled the cauldron, no matter how much she tried to empty it.

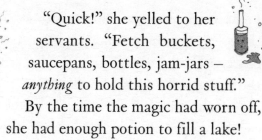

"Quick!" she yelled to her servants. "Fetch buckets, saucepans, bottles, jam-jars — *anything* to hold this horrid stuff."

By the time the magic had worn off, she had enough potion to fill a lake!

Now Morbrecia had also acquired Zorgan's crystal ball. Early on Midsummer's Day, as she was peering into the magical sphere she saw the Silversmith with Sesame, arriving on Mount Fortuna.

"Spallah!"* exclaimed Morbrecia. "Sesame is back and she's brought the bracelet!"

As usual, Morbrecia's doll, Elmo, was sitting nearby. Elmo possessed supernatural powers and now words tumbled from her mouth:

"Twelve charms she has, so you must scheme
To lure her here, then wait unseen.
A scary spider you shall be
Let's set a trap for Sesame!"

"What a good idea!" said Morbrecia, who needed no further encouragement. The thought of turning herself into a spider again was thrilling. It was how it had all started — Morbrecia the spider, stealing the charm bracelet from her sister. "I have the spell books.

* *

* Spallah — excellent! A triumphant expression

35

I have the know-how. Only this time I'll be stealing the bracelet from Sesame. The chance to snatch the bracelet is too good to miss! And then there's only the thirteenth charm to find . . ."

Wafting through an open window, Morbrecia caught a whiff of rotting fish. She looked out to see three gribblers, Varg, Gorz and Bod, scuttling across the bridge to her castle. Every now and then a skreel* leapt from the lake to snap at their heels.

"What do you want?" yelled Morbrecia, holding a hanky over her nose.

"We've got shumshing for you Morbreeesha," said Varg, holding up the tiny silver key. The charm shimmered with a light of its own in the morning sun.

"Vixee!"** cried Morbrecia, punching the air. "Come in."

She couldn't believe her luck. On the very day Sesame had arrived with the bracelet, the gribblers had brought her the last lost charm. She held the key, turning it this way and that, admiring its filigree design.

* *
* Skreel – small flesh-eating fish
**Vixee – a gleeful, triumphant exclamation meaning 'great' or 'wicked'

"Soon *I* shall be queen!" cried Morbrecia to her servants. They were exhausted from filling every available bucket and bottle with smelly potion, and had stopped to have a rest.

The gribblers sniffed the air with their warty noses.

"Lovely pong," said Gorz.

"Mmm!" said Bod. "Something smells delicious."

"What ish it?" asked Varg.

"Um, it's a potion—" began Morbrecia, an idea suddenly whizzing into her head.

"POSHUN!" said Varg, showering everyone with spit. "What short of poshun?"

"Oh," said Morbrecia, thinking quickly. "It makes you strong. Clever. And it helps you see in the dark!"

The gribblers dribbled with eager anticipation.

Morbrecia tried to hide a smile.

"As a reward for bringing me the charm," she told them, "please take the LOT!"

Seven

Meanwhile, Sesame and the Silversmith had left the tunganoras feasting on leaves in the Silversmith's garden. They were on their way to the Silver Pool to return the goblet to Agapogo. As they walked up the mountain, Sesame found herself chatting easily to her companion.

"I remember the legend of the pool,"✶ she said.

* *

✶ Do you remember the intriguing legend? You can read about it in Book Two: *The Silver Pool*

"The gatekeeper, Stanza, told us the story but that was ages ago when I was here with Maddy. She's my best friend, by the way. We felt SO sorry for the dragon. Poor thing! Imagine drowning in a pool of silver . . ."

The Silversmith smiled. Sesame was just as she'd imagined – friendly, caring, inquisitive and fun.

"I *think* you found the horseshoe charm that day?" she said.

"Yes!" said Sesame, and suddenly the perfect little horseshoe reminded her of Silver, far away; and then she thought of her dad, Jodie, her grandmother – everyone she loved – preparing for her birthday party at home. For a split second she was torn between her determination to finish her quest and her longing to be there. She said quietly, almost to herself: "It's my birthday today."

"Ah," said the Silversmith. "I *knew* today was special for you too. Happy Birthday, Sesame!"

When they reached the pool, Sesame looked over the edge. Below them swirled a whirlpool of shimmering silver.

"Oh!" she gasped. "It's amazing."

"I made the magical charms from this pool," said the Silversmith. "It refills itself, no matter how much is used. It's a precious resource, so I try to use it wisely."

Sesame nodded, trying to take it all in. She thought the Silversmith must be very skilful. Fingering the charm bracelet in her pocket, she felt the charms warm and tingly to her touch. Is it, Sesame wondered, because they're close to the Silversmith, the one who made them? There were so many questions she wanted to ask, but now wasn't the time. The Silversmith was preparing to summon the dragon spirit!

Feeling scared, not knowing what to expect, Sesame clutched the goblet so tightly, her knuckles turned white. Fascinated, she watched the Silversmith close her eyes and sway, putting herself into a trance and softly chanting . . .

"Apost, Snargal, Incendus, Agapogo!"

Without warning, a terrifying wind got up and the force of it nearly knocked the two of them off their feet. Sesame braced herself against the blast. When she dared to look, she let out a startled cry.

40

The ghostly vision of Agapogo rose from the pool, her massive wings spread like sails, silvery scales glinting in the morning light.

"Don't be afraid," the Silversmith assured Sesame. "Agapogo will not harm you." She spoke in hushed tones and addressed the phantom respectfully:

"I bring good news," she said. "This is Sesame Brown. She is returning your stolen property."

41

Sesame gulped and took a step forward. The dragon spirit looked awesome! But she took a deep breath and held out the shining silver goblet.

"I th-th-think this b-b-belongs to you," she said. "I t-t-took it from the gribblers—"

Agapogo's hollow eyes lit up like hot coals at the sight of her long lost goblet. She snorted filling the air with scalding steam.

"Throw the goblet to her," said the Silversmith.

So Sesame tossed the goblet and Agapogo caught it in a claw; then the dragon spoke, her voice warm and gentle as a summer breeze:

"Good Silversmith and Sesame,
Kindred spirits in you, I see.
The thirteenth charm this day you'll find,
To evermore the bracelet bind.
A bond forever, as yours shall be –
Good Silversmith and Sesame!"

She sank into the silvery whirlpool, leaving a trace of bubbles on the surface. For a moment, Sesame and the Silversmith stood speechless, their feelings of happiness mixed with sadness. The dragon's words had given them hope for the future and Sesame was *sure* she would find the last charm – although she had no idea where to start looking . . .

The reflection of a doll suddenly appeared in one silvery bubble, which caught her eye. The Silversmith saw it too, and a shiver of fear ran down her spine.

"Quisto!"* she exclaimed. "It's Elmo!"

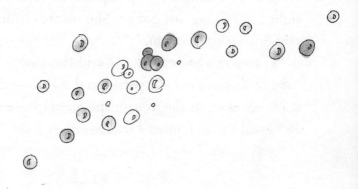

Eight

"Who's Elmo?" asked Sesame. She guessed this was a clue from Agapogo, but what did it mean?

"The doll belongs to Morbrecia," said the Silversmith, and quickly told Sesame all she knew.

"A *magic* doll!" said Sesame, gazing at Elmo in wonder. "Perhaps Elmo knows where the key is. I must go to Morbrecia's castle and find out!"

"It's dangerous," warned the Silversmith. "Morbrecia has taken possession of Zorgan's most powerful spell books. Goodness knows what mischief she's up to! Wait. I'll go with you."

Sesame hesitated. She didn't know why, but suddenly she felt wary of the Silversmith.

"Er, thanks," she said. "But I have to do this on my own. I'm a Charmseeker, remember!"

"I understand," said the Silversmith gently. "But give the charm bracelet to me.

44

It would be dreadful if Morbrecia got hold of it. I'll meet you later at the palace."

The Silversmith's words struck Sesame like a bolt of lightning. *Give the charm bracelet to me.* She'd heard them before – in a NIGHTMARE! In it, Sesame had trusted a beautiful stranger, who'd looked just like the Silversmith. When she gave *her* the precious bracelet, she'd turned into a wicked witch!

Sesame didn't wait a second longer. Without a word, she ran from the Silver Pool and down the mountainside, faster than she'd ever run before.

The Silversmith sighed as she watched Sesame go. There was evil in the air, she could smell it!

Sesame didn't stop running until she'd reached the edge of the Dark Forest. She'd spotted Morbrecia's castle not far away; it loomed eerily out of the early morning mist, from an island in the middle of a lake. Sesame remembered the lake only too well — she and Maddy had once escaped the gribblers by racing across it on giant moon-lilies, dodging the deadly skreels!

She was about to set off again, when she heard the faintest flutter of wings behind her. Thinking it might be Zorgan's pixies, Nix and Dina, out to make trouble for her, Sesame spun round to confront them. However she was relieved to find herself face to face with a fairy, wearing a gown spun from fine cobweb. It was Quilla.

"Fairday,* Seeker," said Quilla, smiling sweetly.

Sesame thought she recognised the fairy and tried to remember where they'd met. Quilla knew what she was thinking.

"The market at Lantern Hill,"** she said. "You stopped to help me."

* *
* **Fairday** – a typical Karisman friendly greeting
** **Lantern Hill** – Do you remember what happened? You can read about it in Book Three: *The Dragon's Revenge*

46

"Quilla!" said Sesame, remembering. "A horrid troll set off a firecracker and you dropped a tray of potions. You gave me a pot of Vanishing Cream."

"Yes," said Quilla. "It helped you escape from Morbrecia."

They looked across to Morbrecia's castle.

"I'm on my way to see her now," said Sesame. "She may know something about the key charm. I must find it."

Quilla gave Sesame a knowing smile.

"Morbrecia is much misunderstood," she said. "Listen. I'll tell you a story, before you go.

"When Morbrecia was a child,
Zorgan's magic made her wild.
He took the princess for a fool –
Tricked her with his plans to rule.
So she, a spider, crept unseen
And stole the bracelet from the queen.
The plan went wrong. The charms were lost!
Now all Karisma bears the cost.
Go, Seeker, and you shall see,
Where the princess keeps the key!"

Before Sesame could thank her, Quilla disappeared. The fairy had simply vanished.

Nine

Midsummer's Day was a holiday in Karisma, as the Silversmith had told Sesame, and each year Queen Charm gave a Garden Party to celebrate. Invitations had been sent to all the guests, including the queen's twelve Gatekeepers. They had permission to leave their posts on this special occasion. Karismans travelled from far and wide to attend the party, and Charm welcomed this opportunity to get to know her subjects better.

The royal gardeners had been busy for weeks – planting flowerbeds, sweeping paths and clipping the huge topiary hedge. There were thirteen topiaries,

each one representing a charm on the queen's bracelet.

One gardener had even remembered to place a fresh pot of poppies in the middle of the maze. By Midsummer's Day, the gardens were looking their very best.

However, on the morning of the party, when the Silversmith arrived at the palace, she was far too anxious to notice the gardens. After Sesame's hasty departure from the Silver Pool, she had hurried to seek Charm's advice.

"I fear Sesame may be in great danger, Your Majesty," she said, wringing her hands. "She has your bracelet—"

"Oh!" cried Charm. She was thrilled to hear about her bracelet, but much more concerned for Sesame. "Where is she? What's happening?"

After the Silversmith told her everything, Charm took charge of the situation.

"Sesame must be protected from Morbrecia," she said. "My sister will do anything to get hold of my bracelet! And if she *does* know where the key is . . ." Charm twisted a strand of fair hair round her finger, contemplating the terrible consequences of Morbrecia in possession of the magical bracelet and *all* its charms.

"I'll send Dork to her castle at once!"

"I will go with him," said the Silversmith.

Party Time!

The twelve gatekeepers have been invited to Queen Charm's garden party. Can you send the right invitation to each gatekeeper?

Etok, Cape Cat
Ramora, Star Island
Troll, The Dark Forest
Hesta, Heartmoor
Feenix, Lantern Hill
Quinch, Shell Beach
Pogg, Butterfly Bay
Stanza, River Two Moons
Ice Maiden, The Ice Country
Bogal, The Swamps
Selena, Mermaid Rock
Pogo, A Cave near The Coins

Solution: 1 Troll; 2 Stanza; 3 Feenix; 4 Etok; 5 Pogg; 6 Bogal; 7 Ice Maiden; 8 Pogo; 9 Ramora; 10 Selena; 11 Quinch; 12 Hesta

Sesame ran across the bridge to the castle. Every now and then she caught a whiff of rotting fish and looked nervously around for the gribblers, but there wasn't a sign of them anywhere. Sesame guessed they *had* been there but had gone, leaving their awful stench behind.

The castle door was wide open, so she stepped inside. What she saw next took her by surprise. In the great flag-stoned hall of the castle servants, coachmen and footmen stood around like statues – frozen as if they'd been playing some weird game of 'move and you're out'. Sesame went up to a guard and stood right in front of him.

"Hi!" she said, waving at him. "Anyone there?"

But there was no reply. The guard stared back, unblinking, as if she wasn't there. Spooky, thought Sesame, and her stomach turned several somersaults – backwards *and* forwards.

She felt alone and very afraid, and wished more than anything that Maddy was with her. And she regretted running away from the Silversmith. *The Silversmith was being so* nice *to me,* she thought miserably. *I don't know what came over me. She must think I'm horrid and—*

A sudden tingling at the nape of her neck jolted Sesame from her daydreaming. She felt her locket. It was unusually warm and the charm bracelet was vibrating – as if the two pieces of jewellery were uniting in their efforts to comfort her.

"Right," said Sesame, pulling herself together. "You're here to look for the key, so hurry up and get on with it. Sesame Brown will track it down!"

She strode across the hall to the foot of a narrow, twisty staircase to the tower and called out:

"Morbrecia! Are you there? It's me, Sesame. I'm coming up."

Her voice echoed round the castle walls. If Morbrecia was there, she wasn't answering. Sesame stepped on the first stair. It creaked. Step by step she went up, one floor after another, higher and higher, until she could go no further. There was one room in the attic and the door was ajar . . .

Sesame went in. The room was small and had a low-beamed ceiling tucked under the eaves; through a window she could see the lake sparkling far below. Everywhere she looked there were spell books, and potions fizzing in jars. A crystal ball was on a stand, and sitting in a rocking chair was Elmo. There was no sign of Morbrecia.

A scuttling sound overhead made Sesame look up at a thick wooden beam. At one end hung a huge cobweb; at the other, sat a spider – watching her every move. Sesame froze and words from Quilla's story flew into her head: *So she, a spider, crept unseen, and stole the bracelet from the queen . . .*

"Give me the bracelet," said Morbrecia the spider, "or I'll turn you into a fly. And you know what will happen then."

Sesame was terrified. But she wasn't going to give in so easily.

"No," she shouted, backing away. "Never!"

Morbrecia waved a spidery leg at Elmo.

"Now," she ordered. "Sesame, the fly. Ha, ha!"

The doll opened her mouth to cast a spell . . . and there, glistening on her tongue, lay the key!

Sesame gasped and lunged at Elmo shaking her, until the key fell from her lips. Then she flung her from the window. Sesame looked down at the lake and heard a dreadful *SMACK!* as Elmo hit the water. Almost immediately, the lake was alive with skreels, their razor-toothed jaws snapping at the doll. The flesh-eating fish worked themselves into a feeding frenzy, and for several minutes the water frothed and foamed.

Then all was still and quiet, as if nothing had ever happened.

Petrified, Sesame turned to look for the spider, but she wasn't there. Instead, standing in the room was Morbrecia – smiling and holding the key. Morbrecia felt as if she'd woken after a strange dream, although she couldn't remember much about it.

"Here," said Morbrecia the princess. "This belongs on Charm's bracelet!"

Ten

"Sesame!" came a shout from the stairs. It was followed by the sound of running feet and shortly afterwards, Officer Dork came into the room, puffing and panting.

"Are you all right, Sesame Brown?" asked Dork. "Princess Morbrecia, I'm arresting you for—"

Sesame stood protectively between Dork and Morbrecia, and behind Dork, she saw the Silversmith.

"It's okay," she said quietly. "Morbrecia and I are friends."

"Wha—?" began Dork.

The Silversmith gave a sigh of relief, happy to find her Seeker safe and Morbrecia back to her normal self. She had seen Elmo fall from the tower and with her, the last evil influence over Morbrecia. The princess was free at last.

"I understand," she said simply.

"I don't," said Dork, baffled. "Girls, eh!"

"I'll tell you later," whispered the Silversmith.

Sesame looked at the Silversmith, seeing now only her true nature. She would never doubt this kind and gentle person again. There was no need to explain; the Silversmith's smiling eyes told Sesame she knew exactly what she was thinking.

Feeling she could burst with happiness, Sesame quickly blinked away tears and fished in her pocket for the charm bracelet. Morbrecia, Dork and the Silversmith gathered round, as she fastened the beautiful filigree key to the silver band. For the first time since Zorgan cast the charms away on that fateful day, so many medes ago, all thirteen magical charms were together again!

"Three cheers for the charms!"

"Spallah!"

"Vixee!"

"Party time, I think," said the Silversmith. "Queen Charm is longing to meet you, Sesame. And she'll be over the two moons to have her bracelet back!"

"I can't wait to meet her," said Sesame.

"And I'm longing to see my sister again," said Princess Morbrecia. "I've missed her."

Morbrecia aimed a swift kick at Curses Ancient and Modern, which happened to be lying at her feet. "I won't be needing these spell books any more!"

A sudden breeze got up and ruffled the pages of the leather-bound tome. Then an odd thing happened; letters and words floated off the pages and out of the window like a swarm of flies. It was the same with all the other books from Zorgan's library. Chants, spells, jinxes and curses jumbled together and disappeared into thin air.

59

Meanwhile, down in the great hall, there came the sound of cheers and a great commotion. Morbrecia's servants had suddenly woken from a sleeping curse and were hurrying about their duties.

"Er, we should be getting back to the palace," said Dork. "Her Majesty's guests are arriving for the Garden Party."

"Yes," said the Silversmith. "Time to be off."

"We can all fit in my carriage," said Morbrecia. But as they turned to go, Sesame caught sight of the crystal ball; she'd never used one and thought it might be fun. Morbrecia guessed what she was thinking.

"Have a go!" she said.

"Who do you wish to see?" asked the Silversmith, although she already knew the answer.

"My friends!" said Sesame excitedly. "They're coming to *my* party today. I wish they could be here to see the bracelet. They helped find the charms too. We're all Charmseekers!"

"I'll see what I can do . . ." said the Silversmith mysteriously.

Eleven

While guests were arriving at the palace for the queen's Garden Party, far away in the Outworld, Sesame's guests were arriving for her disco.

Maddy, Gemma and Liz arrived together early, and had thoughtfully collected Hayley on the way. The four girls squeezed into Mrs Webb's car, then chattered non-stop to Sesame's house about their sparkly outfits, bags, shoes and hair clips.

"Phew!" sighed Maddy's mother, when she dropped them off. "You'd all win gold medals for chatting in the Olympics! Have fun."

Jodie greeted them at the door. She'd been

helping Lossy with party food and had floury hands.

"Go on up to Sesame's room," she said. "She's been getting ready for *ages*. Tell her to hurry up."

They found the room in a mess, with Sesame's clothes all over the floor. Maddy was quick to spot the open jewellery box by her bed. She looked inside and gasped. The charm bracelet had gone – and so, it seemed, had Sesame.

"Ses!" she called out anxiously, looking around.

"What's the matter?" asked Hayley, who knew nothing about the bracelet, the Charmseekers or Karisma.

"Er, nothing," mumbled Maddy, not wanting to alarm their new friend.

"She's probably gone to the loo," said Liz.

"She'll be back in a minute," said Gemma.

But as the four girls sat on Sesame's bed to wait, the strangest things started to happen. First, the room filled with a golden glow, as if lit by magical

candlelight. Next, the girls felt light-headed and, before they knew what was happening, they found themselves floating above the bed and drifting up to the ceiling.

"Whoooooooah!" cried Hayley. "I'm flying."

"Me too," said Maddy, taking her hand. "Hold tight, Hayley. I've a weird feeling we're off to Karisma!"

Officer Dork escorted Princess Morbrecia and Sesame to the Garden Party in Morbrecia's carriage. The Silversmith had suddenly slipped away, promising to meet them at the palace.

"The Silversmith is a mysterious one," said Morbrecia. "She's my sister's best friend but even Charm will never understand her peculiar ways."

"I like her," said Sesame.

"So do I," said Morbrecia. "She has special powers and uses them wisely." She paused for a moment before adding mischievously: "Maybe the Silversmith could teach me a trick or two!"

The four girls floated on golden sunbeams and landed, light as feathers, on their feet. They were in the heart of a circular maze, and in the middle stood a pot of bright, red poppies. The Silversmith was there to greet them.

"Fairday, Charmseekers!" she said. "You're just in time for the party."

"Oh," said Hayley, feeling confused and excited at the same time. "Will someone *please* tell me what's going on?"

"Tell you later," said Maddy.

"Promise," said Gemma.

"Everything," said Liz.

They followed the Silversmith out of the maze, along narrow paths, round and round . . . until they came to the entrance and stepped into the palace gardens. A carriage had just drawn up, and out stepped Princess Morbrecia and Sesame. Maddy would have dashed through the flowerbeds to hug her, but the Silversmith gently held her back.

"All in good time," she whispered.

So they waited patiently, while Sesame knelt before Queen Charm (wobbling only slightly) and presented her with the bracelet.

"Sesame Brown!" exclaimed Charm, taking the bracelet and holding it up for everyone to see. "We meet at last. Your quest is over. You have shown great courage and faced many dangers to bring me my bracelet. You have saved Karisma! Thank you, Sesame. Well done!"

Just then the Silversmith stepped forward.

"Your Majesty," she said. "May I present Maddy, Gemma, Liz and Hayley. They're Charmseekers too and have all played a part in finding your charms."

Sesame was SO surprised to see her friends she let out a yell of delight. But there was so much cheering from the party guests that no one seemed to notice.

"Three cheers for the Charmseekers! Hip, hip, hooray!"

Then Charm turned to Morbrecia and the two sisters embraced.

"We're sisters," said Charm warmly. "From now on we must be friends too!"

"Yes," agreed Morbrecia. "We have *so* much to talk about!"

Dork was standing to attention nearby. Girls, eh, he thought. How they love to gossip!

Sesame glanced at her watch. Before when she'd come to this magical world, her watch had switched to Karisma time. But not now; the display showed 18:50.

"Help!" cried Sesame. "*My* party starts in ten minutes. We must go."

"And so you shall," said the Silversmith. "I'll make sure you arrive in time. But first, Her Majesty wishes to give you these tokens of our appreciation."

For Maddy, Gemma, Liz and Hayley, the Silversmith had made friendship bands, and to each was attached a silver heart, inscribed with their initial. And for Sesame, her special Seeker, there was a bracelet, which *looked* just like Charm's magical bracelet – with thirteen silver charms!

The Charmseekers were thrilled and put them on at once. Then everyone joined in and sang The Song of Charms and cheered the girls again and again.

"Thirteen charms on a silver band,
United hold our world in hand.
May this gift for good Queen Charm,
Keep Karisma safe from harm.
One and all, beware the day
Charms and bracelet break away.
Together they must always stay!"

After many more goodbyes and fond farewells, it was time for the girls to leave. They were never quite sure how it happened, but suddenly they were flying through time and space in a golden haze of stars, until THUMP, BUMP, THUMP, BUMP, THUMP! – five girls landed in a giggling heap, back on Sesame's bed.

Jodie and Nic popped their heads round the door.

"It's seven o'clock," said Jodie.

"Everything's ready," said Nic.

And through Sesame's bedroom window came the beat of Crystal Chix. It was going to be a great birthday party!

Twelve

M uch later that night, after everyone had gone home, Sesame sat in her room and talked to her teddy, Alfie.

"I've had the best day ever," she told him. "So much has happened, I can't believe it's all true."

She looked at the photographs of Silver, her very own pony, and of Kee-Kee the orangutan she would help to support, thanks to her grandmother Lossy. She'd had a fantastic disco and made lots of new friends – and soon she'd have a new mum too. Jodie and her dad were very happy together, and she loved them both.

And then there was Karisma! How would she begin to tell her family about that wonderful magical world and all the friends she'd made there? Her quest had meant so much to her and now it had come to an end.

"I *will* tell them," she said. "Tomorrow. I'll tell them everything in the morning." She stifled a yawn and stretched. "But tonight I'm much too tired!"

Sesame unfastened the charm bracelet — *her* charm bracelet — and put it in the jewellery box, where she would always keep it. Then she took off her necklace, and felt it warm and tingly to her touch. For one startling moment, Sesame thought something unusual might happen — and in a way it did. She opened her locket and looked fondly at the tiny pictures of her parents — Nic and Poppy. Then, as she looked at her mother, she thought she saw for the very first time a resemblance between the Silversmith and Poppy. It made her happy to think there was someone far away in another world like her mother . . .

Sesame closed her locket and placed it in the jewellery box, next to her bracelet. It was then she noticed the engraving on the back of her locket.

It was her initial 'S'.

Thirteen

The Silversmith sighs contentedly. Her Seeker's quest is over. The last magic candle has long since flickered and gone out. The precious charm bracelet has been returned to Queen Charm, and soon all will be well in Karisma.

The two moons of Karisma rise over Mount Fortuna and in the velvet night sky, the Silversmith looks at a bright star and thinks of Sesame. Perhaps across the vastness of time and space, her Seeker will see it too.

Acknowledgments

I owe a debt of gratitude to all those who have worked behind the scenes at Orion Children's Books and beyond to bring the *Charmseekers* books and their thirteen delightful charms to you. Since it would take more space than this edition allows to mention individuals by name, suffice it to say that I'm hugely grateful to my publishers and everyone involved with the publication of this series. In particular, my special thanks go to: my publisher, Fiona Kennedy, for her faith in believing I could write way beyond my own expectations. Her creative, tactful and skilful editing kept Sesame Brown on the right track and helped me to write a better story; my agent, Rosemary Sandberg; Jenny Glencross and Jane Hughes (Editorial); Alex Nicholas and Helen Speedy (Rights) Loulou Clark and Helen Ewing (Design); Clare Hennessy (Production); Jessica Killingley and Jo Dawson (Marketing); Pandora White (Orion Audio Books); Imogen Adams (Website designer – www.hammerinheels.com); Neil Pymer, the *real* Spinner Shindigs, for kind permission to use his name; and last, but by no means least, a million thanks go to my husband Tom for his inexhaustible patience, critical appraisal and support along the way.

Georgie Adams